Numbers 1-10

Press out stickers, moisten,
and place them on the pages
where they belong.

page 31

 one

 two

 three

 four

 five

 six

 seven   eight

1 one

Trace the number. Write it on the line.

Find the sticker with the number 1.
Put it on the [____].

Put a sticker here.

2 two

Trace the number. Write it on the line.

Find the sticker with the number 2.
Put it on the [   ].

Put a sticker here.

3 three

Trace the number. Write it on the line.

3 3   3

Find the sticker with the number 3.
Put it on the ⬚.

Put a sticker here.

4 four

Trace the number. Write it on the line.

Find the sticker with the number 4.
Put it on the [ ].

Put a sticker here.

Skills: recognizing and writing the numeral 4; counting four objects

Find the 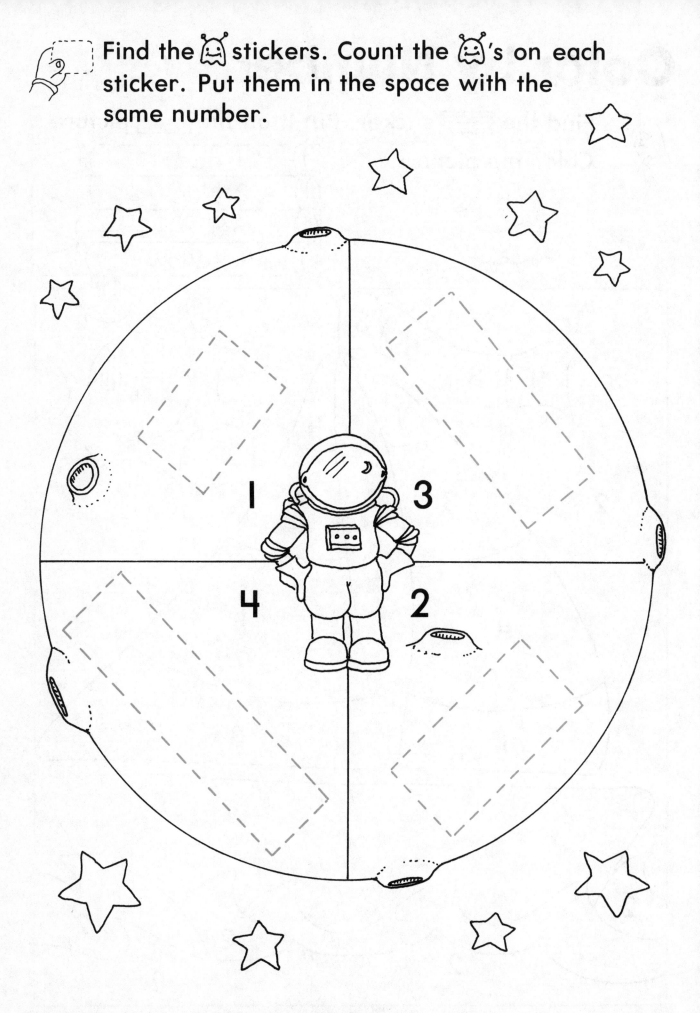 **stickers. Count the 's on each sticker. Put them in the space with the same number.**

1

3

4

2

Color by Number

Find the ☰☰ sticker. Put it on the [ ] picture.
Color the picture.

1	red
2	blue
3	green
4	yellow

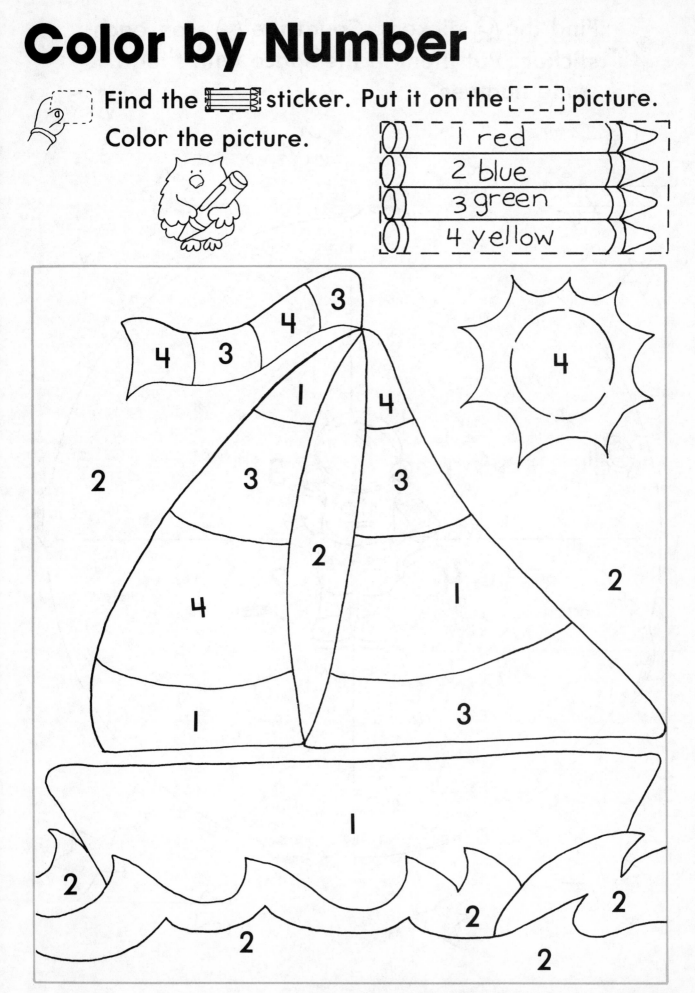

Skill: completing a picture by using a color code

5 five

Trace the number. Write it on the line.

5 5

Find the sticker with the number 5.
Put it on the ☐.

Put a sticker here.

Count the objects in each set.
Trace the numbers.

Skill: recognizing and tracing the numerals 1-5

Matching

Draw a line from the 2 to the sets with 2 ☆.

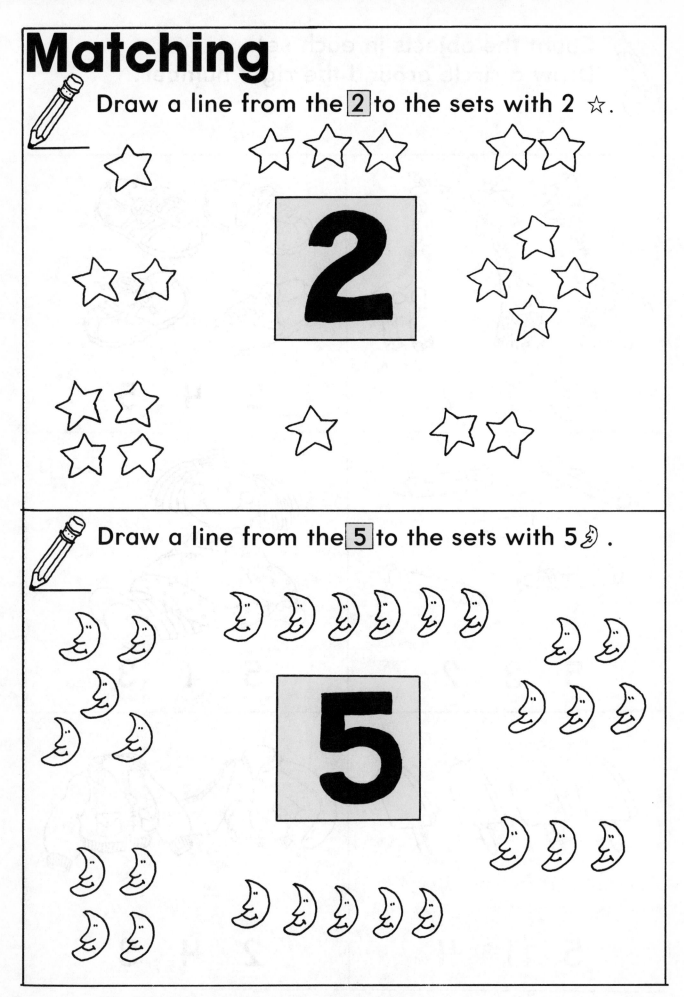

Draw a line from the 5 to the sets with 5 🌙.

 Count the objects in each set.
Draw a circle around the right number.

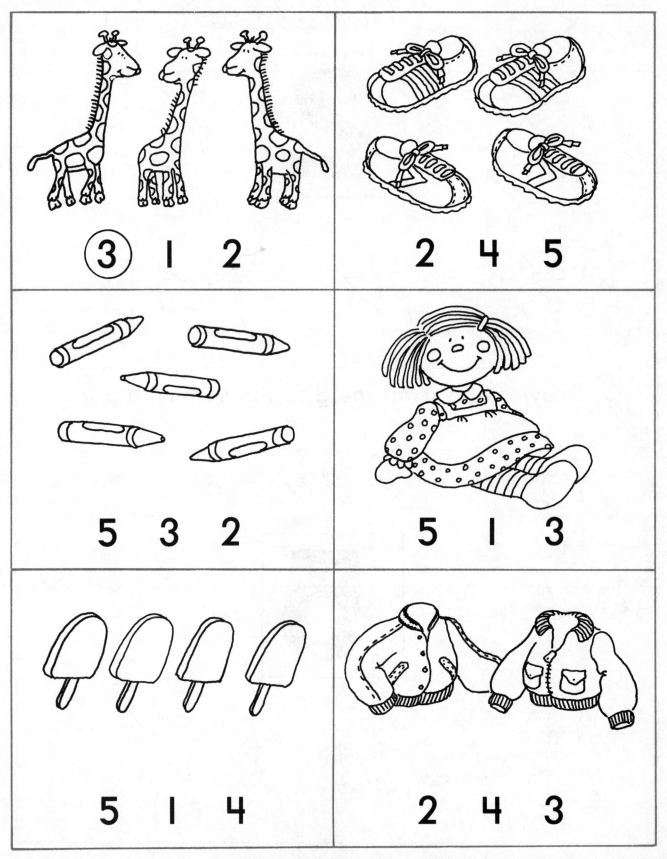

③ 1 2

2 4 5

5 3 2

5 1 3

5 1 4

2 4 3

Skill: matching the number of members in a set to the correct numeral

6 six

Trace the number. Write it on the line.

6 6   6

Find the sticker with the number 6.
Put it on the ☐.

Put a sticker here.

7 seven

Trace the number. Write it on the line.

7

Find the sticker with the number 7.
Put it on the ⬚.

Put a sticker here.

7

Skills: recognizing and writing the numeral 7; counting seven objects

Count the animals in each set.

✂ Cut and paste the right number next to each set of animals.

2 5 7 3

Find the circus stickers. Put them on the pictures.

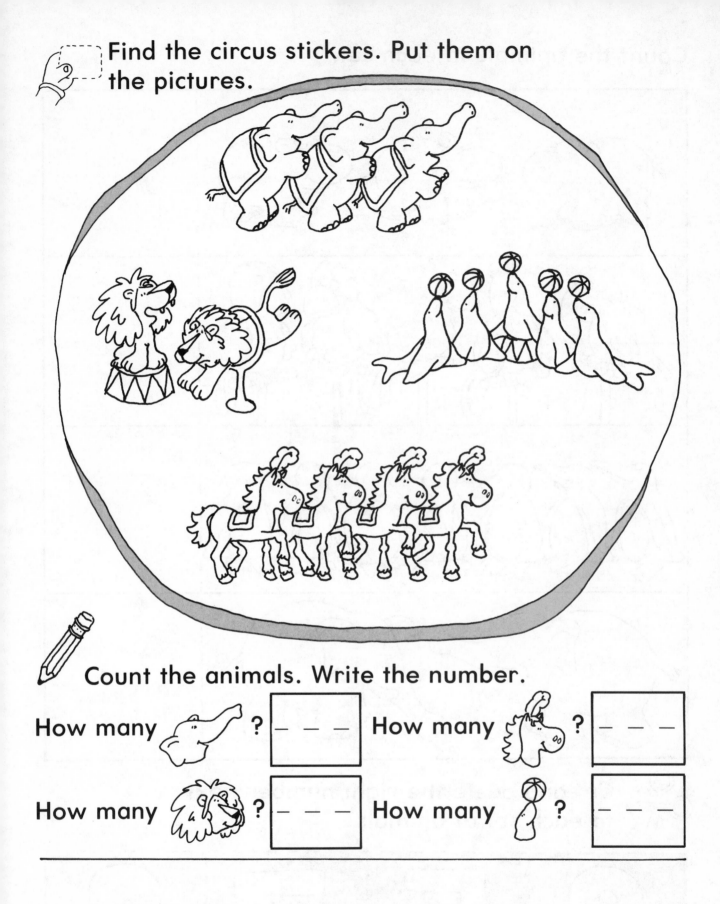

Count the animals. Write the number.

How many ![elephant] ? _ _ _ How many ![horse] ? _ _ _

How many ![lion] ? _ _ _ How many ![seal] ? _ _ _

14

**Look at the number. Count the objects.
Color the right number of objects
in each set.**

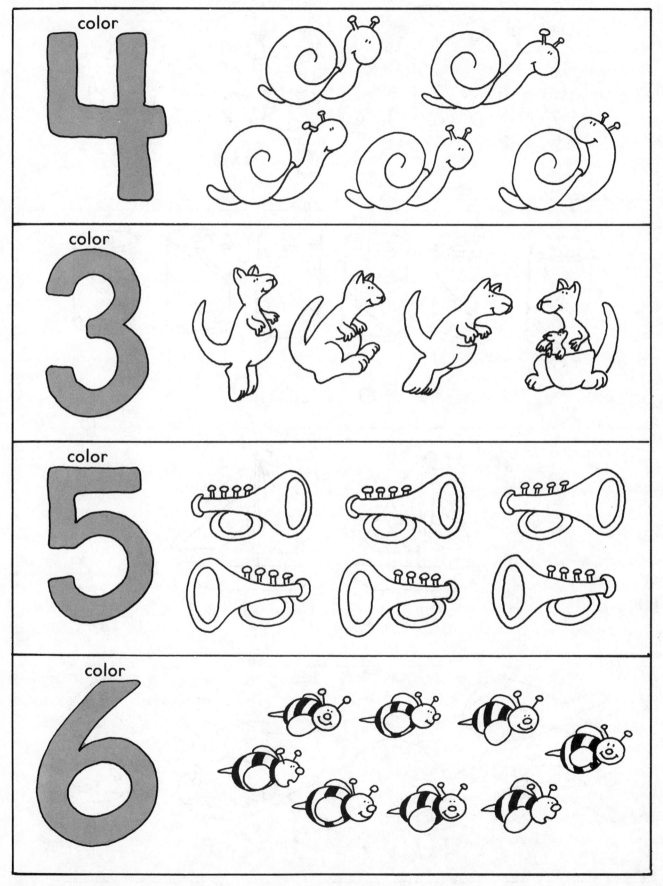

color
4

color
3

color
5

color
6

Count the objects in each set.
Trace the right number.

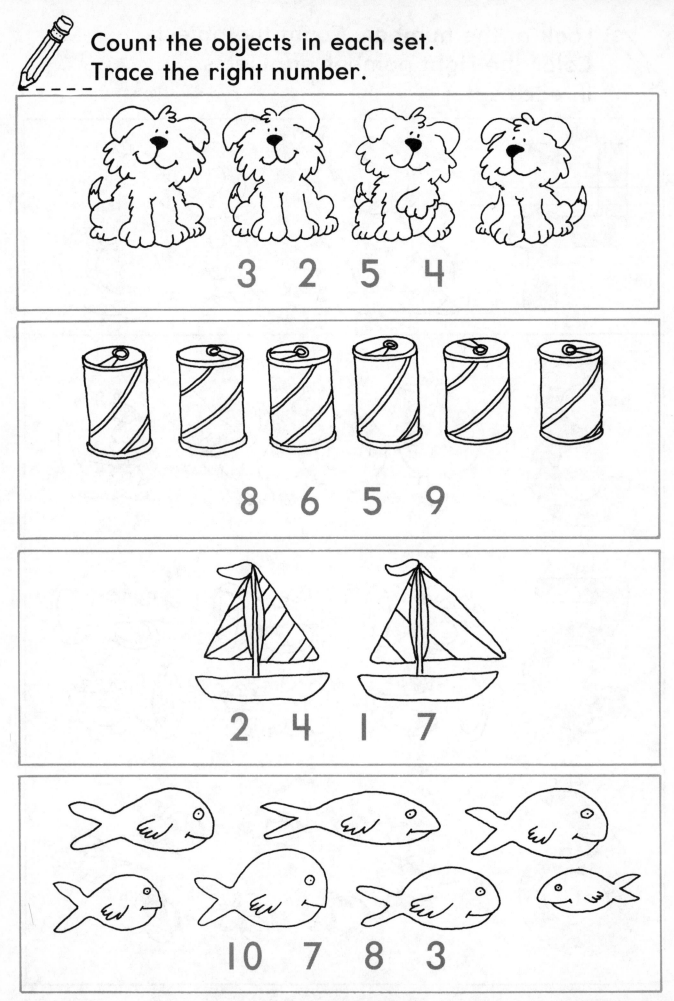

3 2 5 4

8 6 5 9

2 4 1 7

10 7 8 3

Skill: matching the number of members in a set to the correct numeral

8 eight

Trace the number. Write it on the line.

8 8

8

Find the sticker with the number 8.
Put it on the ⌐ ¬.

Put a sticker here.

Count the animals in each set.
Write the number on the line.

How many?

_____

- - - - - - -

_____

How many?

_____

- - - - - - -

_____

How many?

_____

- - - - - - -

_____

<u>Skill</u>: counting the members in a set and writing the correct numeral

Count the objects in each set.
Write the number on the line.

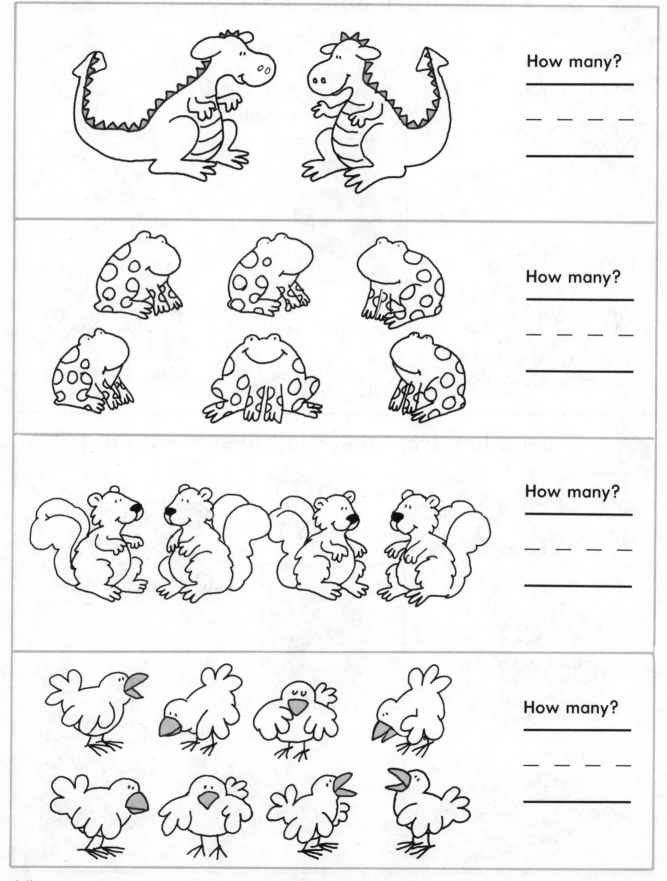

How many?

_____
- - - - -
_____

How many?

_____
- - - - -
_____

How many?

_____
- - - - -
_____

How many?

_____
- - - - -
_____

Skill: counting the members in a set and writing the correct numeral

19

Matching

Draw a line from the 6 to the sets with 6 🌷 .

6

Draw a line from the 8 to the sets with 8 🐝 .

8

Skill: matching a numeral to sets with the same number of members

9 nine

Trace the number. Write it on the line.

Find the sticker with the number 9.
Put it on the ☐.

Put a sticker here.

10 ten

Trace the number. Write it on the line.

Find the sticker with the number 10.
Put it on the ☐.

Put a sticker here.

Skills: recognizing and writing the numeral 10; counting ten objects

Count the objects in each set.
Write the number on the line.

1 2 3 4 5 6 7 8 9 10

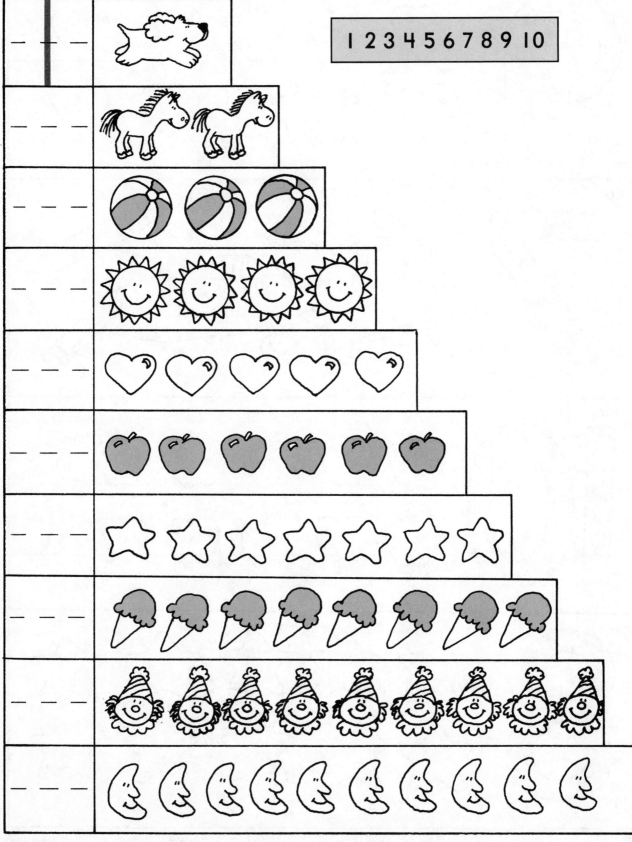

Look at the number. Count the objects.
Color the right number of objects in each set.

Skill: coloring the correct number of members to complete a specific set

1 2 3 4 5 6 7 8 9 10

Count the objects in each set.
Draw a circle around the right number.

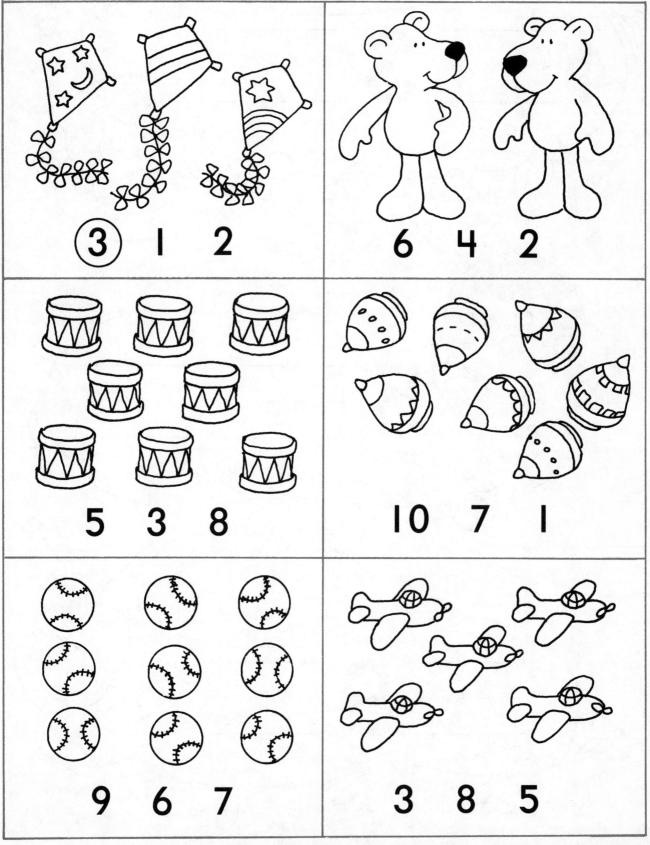

(3) 1 2

6 4 2

5 3 8

10 7 1

9 6 7

3 8 5

Skill: matching the number of members in a set to the correct numeral

Matching

 Draw a line from each number to the set with the same number of objects.

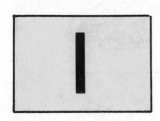

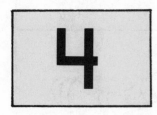

Count the objects in each set.
Write the number on the line.

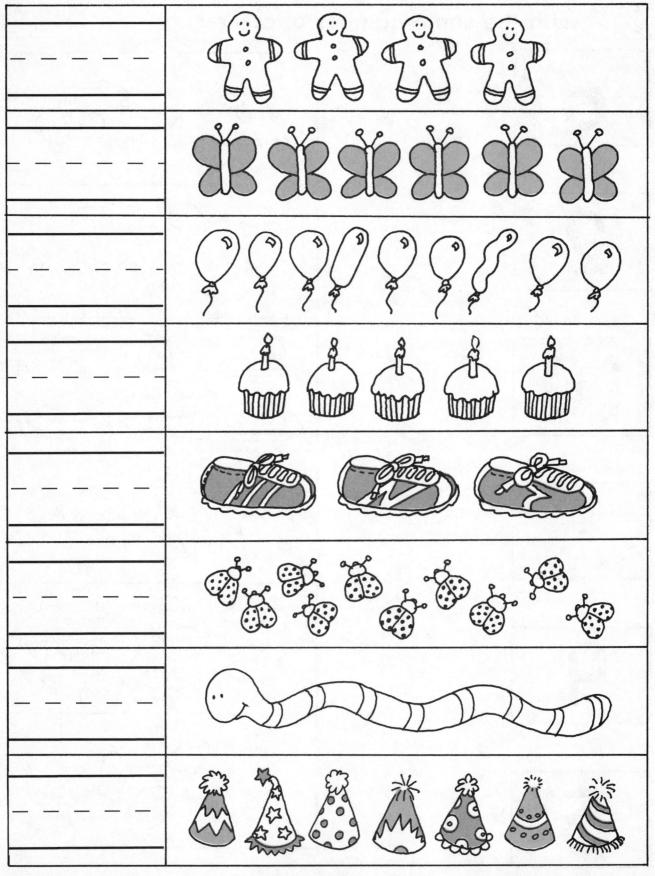

Skill: counting the members of a set and writing the correct numeral

Start at 1. Count the numbers in order to 10. Draw a line to connect the dots.

Find the numbers hidden in the picture. Draw a circle around them.

Skill: recognizing the numerals 1-10

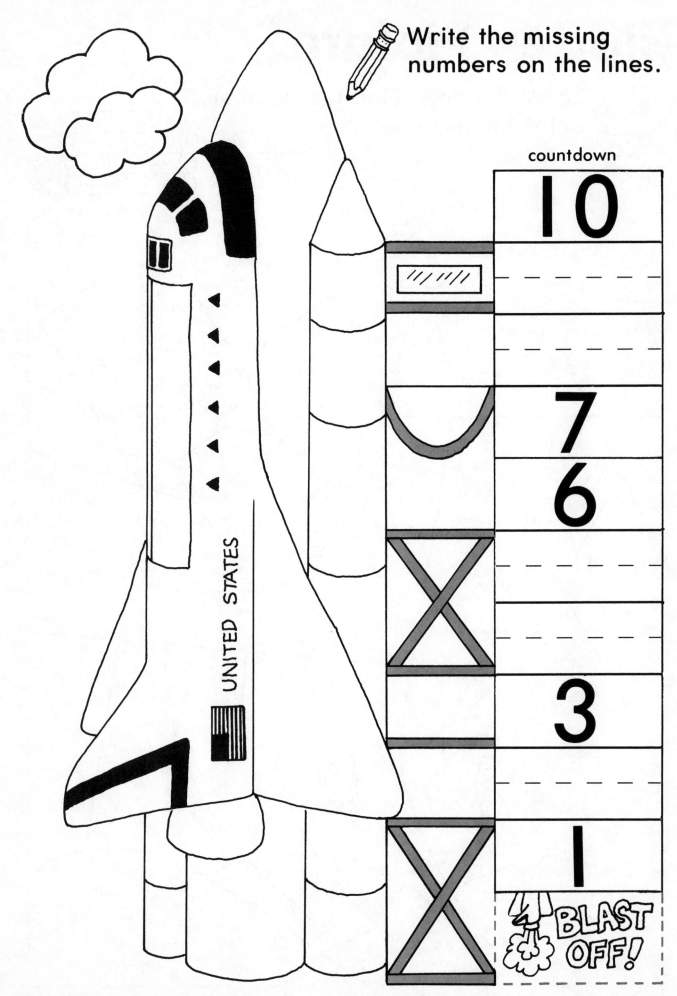

Write the missing
numbers on the lines.

countdown

10

_ _ _

_ _ _

7

6

_ _ _

_ _ _

3

_ _ _

1

BLAST
OFF!

Hidden Picture

Count the dots. Find the number.
Color the picture.

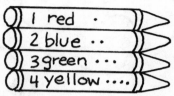

1 red	·
2 blue	··
3 green	···
4 yellow	····

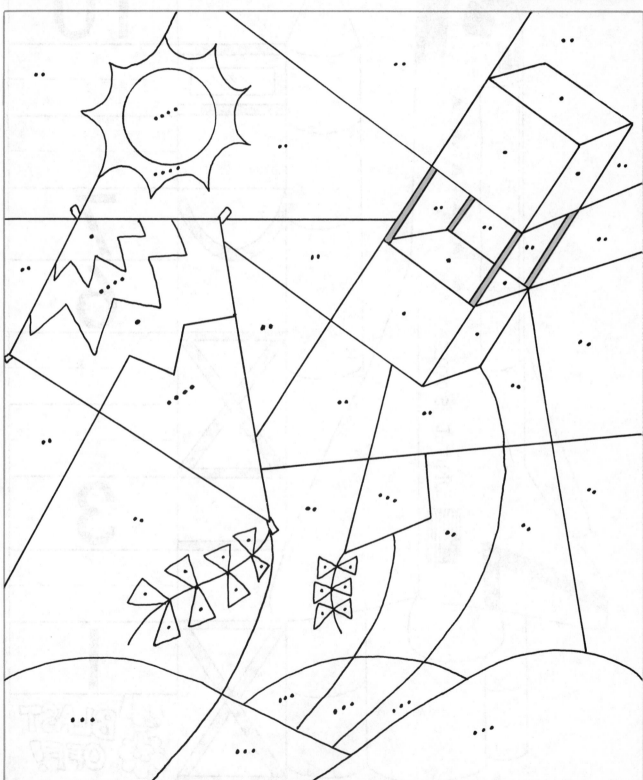

Skill: completing a picture by using a color code

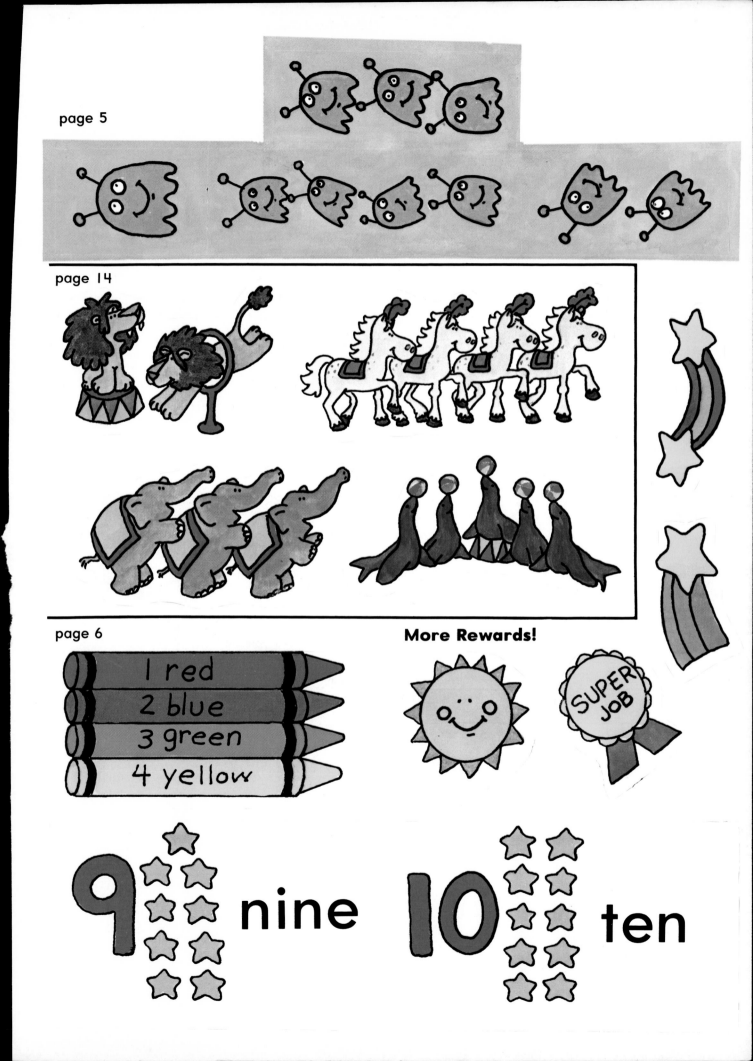

page 5

page 14

page 6

1	red
2	blue
3	green
4	yellow

More Rewards!

SUPER JOB

9 nine

10 ten